PROFILES

Paul McCartney

Alan Hamilton

Illustrated by
Karen Heywood

D0672517

Hamish Hamilton
London

Titles in the Profiles series

Muhammad Ali	0 241 10600 1
Geoffrey Boycott	0 241 10712 1
Charlie Chaplin	0 241 10479 3
Winston Churchill	0 241 10482 3
Sebastian Coe	0 241 10848 9
Thomas Edison	0 241 10713 X
.Queen Elizabeth II	0 241 10850 0
Martin Luther King	0 241 10931 0
Paul McCartney	0 241 10930 2
Rudolf Nureyev	0 241 10849 7
Pope John Paul II	0 241 10711 3
Lucinda Prior-Palmer	0 241 10710 5
Kevin Keegan	0 241 10594 3
Lord Mountbatten	0 241 10593 5
Anna Pavlova	0 241 10481 5
Barry Sheene	0 241 10851 9
Mother Teresa	0 241 10933 7
Margaret Thatcher	0 241 10596 X
Daley Thompson	0 241 10932 9
Queen Victoria	0 241 10480 7

First published 1983 by
Hamish Hamilton Children's Books
Garden House, 57-59 Long Acre, London WC2E 9JZ
© text 1983 by Alan Hamilton
© illustrations 1983 by Karen Heywood
British Library Cataloguing in Publication Data
Hamilton, Alan
Paul McCartney.
1. McCartney, Paul   2. Rock music — England —
Biography
I. Title
784.5'40092'4   ML410.M115
ISBN 0-241-10930-2
Typeset by Pioneer
Printed in Great Britain by
Cambridge University Press

Contents

1   One in a Million

Take a million boys and girls, and at some time or another most of them will want to belong to a pop group. It promises to be exciting, glamorous, and enormous fun, and may even earn them lots of money.

Most of them will never get round to it, because they do not have the patience or the skill to learn an instrument, or because they suddenly decide to take an interest in home computers, or hockey, or taking cars to pieces. Out of the original million, perhaps a thousand will persevere, and join an amateur group to play for fun.

That's still a lot of pop groups. And they will all have an ambition to make a record. Out of that thousand, perhaps a hundred will be good enough to attract the interest of a record company who will be prepared to give them a chance.

That's still a lot of records. Many records which are issued never even get played on the radio, and only a very few will find their way into the Top Thirty, perhaps only ten out of the original hundred — which is a tiny number out of our original million.

But that's still a lot of hits. How many of *them* manage to stay at the top, record after record? Let's say half of them, which brings us down to five. And how many of that five can top record charts all over the world, count their record sales in tens of millions, and draw huge audiences to their live concerts everywhere from America to Australia, year after year? Perhaps just two.

And out of the singers in these two groups, how

Performing and songwriting have made Paul one of the richest men in Britain

many can break up their original band, start a completely different one, and be just as successful all over again, selling more records and writing more songs than almost anyone else before?

From our original million, that brings us down to just one, and his name is Paul McCartney.

In the world of popular music, there has never been anyone quite like Paul. Not only has he been one of the most successful performers of pop music, with the Beatles, his own Wings band, and as a solo artist, he has also been one of the most successful writers of pop songs. In fact, Paul has broken almost as many records as he has made. Here are just a few of them.

Records on which Paul has performed have sold at least 300 million copies around the world, of which roughly one third were Beatles singles, one third were Beatles albums, and one third were recorded by Wings or Paul singing solo. Only Bing Crosby and Elvis Presley approach anywhere near that total.

Paul wrote, and performed on, *I Want to Hold Your Hand* by the Beatles, which at 13 million copies worldwide is the biggest selling British record of all time. He also wrote and performed *Mull of Kintyre*, which had the biggest sale ever of any single record in Britain.

In Britain alone, Paul the performer has had 40 records in the Top Ten, 23 with the Beatles, 12 with Wings and 5 on his own.

He has been equally successful as a songwriter, having written either alone or with his former partner John Lennon, 43 songs which have sold a million or more records. His composition *Yesterday* has, besides his own version, been recorded by at least 1,186 other artists, from solo singers to symphony orchestras. No other modern song has been recorded in so many versions.

Naturally, a man who has written and performed so many bestselling songs must be very rich indeed, and Paul is now probably one of the richest men in Britain. Nobody — not even Paul — knows exactly how much he is worth, but his fortune is believed to be approaching £250 million. Every year he earns about £20 million, which is over £50,000 a day.

Of course everyone who earns a lot of money in Britain pays a great deal in tax, and the amount Paul pays back to the Government each year is approximately enough to keep the whole Royal Family going. But despite the crippling taxation, Paul has never wanted to live anywhere but Britain. He was born in Liverpool, and his attachment to his birthplace is still very strong. He has more money than he will ever need, and he can afford to live where he likes, which happens to be his farms in Sussex and Scotland.

Not everything which Paul McCartney has done has been a success. After he left the Beatles, he had his share of bad records which flopped, and he has been arrested several times for possessing drugs. But of all the boys and girls who ever wanted to play in a pop group, Paul remains one in a million.

2 'Maca'

There was always music in the McCartney family, even in the days when record players grew horns like giant ear trumpets and were called gramophones.

Joe McCartney, Paul's grandfather, was an Irishman who was born last century, so long ago that not even gramophones had been invented, and radios had certainly not been thought of, not even the big old ones that glowed in the dark and took long minutes to warm up. The McCartneys had left Ireland because the nineteenth century was a time of famine and hardship in that poor country.

The boats from Ireland sailed to Liverpool, and thousands of poor Irish boarded the boats in search of work, got off at Liverpool, and never went any further. Joe McCartney was one of those Liverpool Irish, who worked in a tobacco factory at Everton. He was a typical Irishman, being very fond of music, and when he was not making tobacco he played in a Territorial Army brass band. In those days, if you wanted music, you made it yourself.

Joe McCartney had a son called James, who fell off a wall when he was a boy, damaging his ear and leaving him partially deaf for the rest of his life. But that did not prevent him from inheriting Grandpa Joe's love of music; he taught himself to play the piano.

Jim became such a good amateur musician that he formed his own band, which was first called the Masked Melody Makers, but then renamed Jim Mac's Band, which he thought sounded better. Jim's job as a salesman at the Liverpool Cotton Exchange was not well paid, and the dance band brought in extra money, especially welcome when he married Mary Mohin, a girl from another Liverpool Irish family and a nurse at the local Walton Hospital.

German bombers were raiding the great sprawling docklands of Liverpool, where much of Britain's vital wartime food supply was landed, on the night of 18 June 1942, when James Paul McCartney was born, barely a couple of kilometres away, in a private ward of his mother's hospital at Walton. The war was at its height, and the great port on Merseyside was a prime target for the waves of bombers which nightly came to shower England with their deadly cargoes. No sooner had Paul been born than the family had to flee their Liverpool home to the safety of a house in Wallasey, across the Mersey away from the attentions of the enemy raiders.

When the war was over, the family, which now numbered four with the arrival of Paul's younger brother Michael, moved back to a house of their own in the Speke district of Liverpool, and Jim McCartney was reunited with his beloved piano. He liked nothing more than to gather the whole McCartney tribe of children, cousins, aunts and uncles round the piano for a good old-fashioned sing-song, like families always used to do in the old days before gramophones.

Paul and his brother went to school round the corner from their home at 72 Western Avenue, Speke. It was properly called Stockton Wood Road Infants' School, but to the children it was just 'Stocky Wood'. When that

Paul was a bright pupil at school, where his friends called him 'Maca'

school became too crowded, Paul had to travel by bus to the Joseph Williams Primary School at Gateacre.

The young McCartney was a bright boy at school. When he was eleven he had no trouble at all in passing his examination to enter the Liverpool Institute High School, one of the best schools in the city. It was such a mouthful of a name that the boys called it simply 'The Inny'; the new boy they called simply 'Maca'.

Jim McCartney was proud of his elder son, and he

was proud of himself too, for he was earning enough money to move his family to bigger and better houses, first to 12 Ardwick Road, Speke, and then to 20 Forthlin Road, Allerton. But there was one disappointment in Jim's life; Paul showed very little sign of becoming musical. Something, Jim decided, would have to be done.

Paul was sent to piano lessons. But he was just like any other boy who is sent to practise the piano when he would rather be kicking a football in the sunshine — he *loathed* it. The piano lessons were soon abandoned. Jim had no better luck with Grandpa Joe's trumpet, which still lay about the house. Paul showed as much interest in that as he had done in the piano.

But in 1956, when Paul was fourteen years old, two things happened which, in their different ways, were to awaken in Paul the old McCartney family talent for making music in a manner that Jim could never have dreamt of.

First, Paul's mother Mary died of cancer quite suddenly after only a short illness. Jim was left to bring up two teenage boys on his own, and Paul became lost and unsettled, as though looking for something to fill the huge gap in his life left by the loss of his mother.

Second, he very soon found what he was looking for. Across the Atlantic from America there came a new and astonishing sound, quite unlike anything anyone in England had ever heard before. Girls screamed with excitement, and parents feared for the safety of their children. It was the sound of rock and roll.

14

3 A Frantic New Rhythm

In the whole history of popular music, there has never quite been a year like 1956.

There were records, of course, the big black kind that turned at 78 r.p.m. and broke if you dropped them. Mostly they featured dance bands, or swing bands, or jazz bands, or singers singing in front of full orchestras. Now suddenly there was a band named Bill Haley and the Comets, playing a song called *Rock Around The Clock* in a frantic new rhythm. It was the birth of rock and roll.

And, almost at the same time, the voice of another new American singer was heard in Britain, unlike anything that had been heard before. His name was Elvis Presley, from Tennessee in the southern United States, and his first hit record was called *Heartbreak Hotel.* Presley sang rock and roll too, but it was different from the bright, chirpy kind of Bill Haley's Comets. Presley's was a wild, angry kind of music, loosely based on 'blues', the kind of songs American black people used to sing when they bemoaned the fact that, nearly a century after the end of the American Civil War which was supposed to end slavery, their lives were sometimes little better than those of slaves.

Britain, like America, went wild over Presley and all the other singers who copied his drooping jaw and swivelling hips. It was nine years since the war had finished, the British were becoming prosperous again, there were plenty of jobs for everyone, and even teenagers had money to spend. They were very soon

Bill Haley and his Comets introduced rock and roll to Britain with
Rock around the Clock

spending it on records, at six shillings (30p) each.

At the same time, another new music craze exploded over Britain. Lonnie Donegan, a singer and banjo player in the Chris Barber Jazz Band, made a record called *Rock Island Line*, in a very simple style of beat music, using simple instruments, known as skiffle.

Now the unusual thing about all three of these performers was that they played guitars. Previously, guitars had been played only by intense Spaniards, or buried deep in the rhythm sections of dance bands. But now they suddenly became a featured instrument. There was no doubt in the fourteen-year-old Paul McCartney's mind: he had to have one. The new music had seized him, as it had seized most of the teenagers in England.

His father did not need to be asked twice; he went straight out and bought Paul a guitar for £15. Then Jim

16

sat down at his beloved piano and taught his son the basic chords.

The new rock and roll was the first kind of music that teenagers could call their own, and the fact that their parents so thoroughly detested it made it all the more precious to them. To assert their independence further, they started dressing in tight trousers and long jackets, based very loosely on the style of clothes worn in Edwardian times, which is why they immediately became known as Teddy Boys.

For Paul, unsettled since his mother's death, the music opened up a whole new world. The guitar became an obsession that filled every spare moment of his day. But at first he found it extraordinarily difficult to play, and he could barely master even the two or three chords needed to play skiffle songs.

Then at last it dawned on Paul what he was doing wrong. For everything else, like writing, he was naturally right-handed, but for playing the guitar he was naturally *left*-handed. From the moment he turned the instrument round and reversed the order of the strings, he made progress.

Learning the new songs was no easy matter. Six shillings for a record was a great deal of money to a fourteen-year-old, and at first the BBC refused to broadcast rock and roll, because they thought it tuneless and wicked. Paul, like thousands of other teenagers of his era, discovered rock and roll under the bedclothes at night, listening secretly to Radio Luxembourg, the Continental station that beamed constant record programmes to rock-starved England.

John Lennon was the biggest influence on Paul's musical life

The following year Jim McCartney took the two boys to Butlin's holiday camp at Filey, Yorkshire, to help younger brother Michael recover from a broken arm. There the two made their first public appearance, entering a talent contest to sing two rock hits of the day, *Bye Bye Love* and *Long Tall Sally*. They did not win the £5,000 prize, which is perhaps just as well as they were under age.

Paul really wanted to join a group. Groups had sprung up everywhere. To play skiffle all you needed was a guitar, your mother's tin washboard for the rhythm section, and a tea chest and broom handle to make a bass. A school friend of Paul's knew of a group that had been formed at another Liverpool high school, Quarry Bank, who called themselves the Quarry Men.

On a summer afternoon in 1957 at a church fete in Woolton, Liverpool, where the Quarry Men had been asked to play, Paul was taken to meet their leader, a rebellious young man who wore drainpipe trousers, and a green silk waistcoat under his blazer. Paul, on the other hand, had been forbidden by his father to wear drainpipes, but every week he would sneak out to a little tailor's shop and have his trousers taken in a fraction at a time until the bottoms were down to the fashionable twelve inches (300-odd centimetres).

'This', said Paul's schoolfriend introducing him to the leader of the Quarry Men, 'is John Lennon'.

4   Crickets and Beetles

At their first meeting, John Lennon was wary of the newcomer. They were so different: John was a rebel from a middle-class home, while Paul was a working-class boy, always polite and eager to please. But Paul possessed one great skill which the Quarry Men badly needed: he was the only one who knew how to tune a guitar.

Paul was very soon invited to join the Quarry Men to play rhythm guitar. Although they were so different, he and John quickly became firm friends; Paul taught John how to improve his guitar playing, and showed him some songs he had been trying to write. John, who had a sharp mind which loved playing with words, suggested changes and improvements.

The Quarry Men became Paul's life. John remained its undisputed leader, but Paul became the only other member who really mattered, because he had much more musical skill than any of the others. Every day after school, and every weekend, he and John would practise until the ends of their fingers were raw from plucking the steel guitar strings.

Jim McCartney thought the new boy who came to his house a very strange character indeed, and did not really approve of Paul mixing with that sort of company. At the same time, he began to worry about his son's school career. From being a bright boy who sailed through his school work with ease, Paul began to lose interest in everything except music. Soon after joining the Quarry Men he sat his O-level examinations

Paul was still at school when he joined John Lennon's group, the Quarrymen

in Spanish and Latin, but failed the Latin. Even so, his father still had high hopes for Paul. He wanted him to pass all his school examinations, go on to college, and become a schoolteacher.

Meanwhile, the Quarry Men had grown bored with skiffle. For anyone really interested in music, it was too simple. England was beginning to produce its own home-grown rock and roll singers like Tommy Steele, and Cliff Richard and the Shadows. Television had decided that rock music was perhaps not such a naughty noise after all, and anyway it was so popular they could not afford to ignore it. Now, every Saturday, there was a rock show called *Oh Boy!* Paul would watch it religiously every week, straining at the screen to see which chords the guitarists played, then cycling over to John Lennon's house to try them out before they were forgotten.

The Quarry Men were becoming well enough known

21

in the district to be hired for occasional dances, including those at the art college next door to Paul's school where John Lennon had enrolled as a student after failing all his school examinations. But they were no better than any of the dozens of other amateur groups in Liverpool. In fact they were so bad that they were sometimes booed off the stage halfway through their act.

But they were very determined. One day in the summer of 1958 they heard of a talent contest being run by Granada Television in Manchester. The Quarry Men, they decided, was an uninspiring name for a group just about to break into stardom, so John Lennon dreamed up the name Johnny and the Moondogs. They took the bus to Manchester, performed their act, but had to leave to catch the last bus home before the results were announced. They missed nothing: the audience did not like them, and they never had any real chance of winning.

Besides owning a coffee bar where the boys would while away long hours over one cup of coffee, Allan Williams was a dance and concert promoter. He took an interest in the Moondogs, and arranged for them to have an audition in front of one of the important London concert agents who was visiting Liverpool, Larry Parnes. Parnes was so rich and successful that he was known as Mr Parnes, Shillings and Pence. He was not very impressed either, but he needed a backing group to join a tour of Scotland with one of his rock stars, Johnny Gentle. Would the Moondogs do it for £18 each? They certainly would.

The early Beatles with their new recruit, George Harrison

Jim McCartney was not at all happy about Paul taking two weeks off when he should have been studying hard for his A-level exams, but Paul had a persuasive tongue, and somehow managed to convince his father that the break from revision would do him good. Jim reluctantly agreed.

Again the group decided they should have a better name. One of their favourite groups was the Crickets, who played with the American singer Buddy Holly. Why not, someone suggested, call themselves after another insect? How about the Beetles? They thought that was a very silly name, but John Lennon, with his love of word play, reminded them that they played beat music, and that to change the spelling to Beatles would be clever and witty.

On their exhausting two-week tour around Scotland John and Paul took with them Stu Sutcliffe, a guitarist

friend of John's from art college; Tommy Moore, who drove a fork lift truck in a bottle factory, and owned a full set of drums; and a sad-eyed butcher's boy who always hung around the group hoping for a chance to play, George Harrison.

Paul returned to sit his A-level exams in art and English, while Tommy Moore, who had hated every minute of the Scottish tour and had fallen out with the rest of the group, took his drums and went back to his fork lift truck, swearing never to have anything to do with the Beatles ever again. It looked as if the Beatles might wind up, for nobody would hire a band without a drummer.

But Allan Williams was still working on their behalf. He had heard that British rock groups were very popular in the German city of Hamburg, and he managed to get the Beatles a booking there, providing

Two of the original Beatles, Pete Best and Stu Sutcliffe, were to leave the group while it was still unknown outside Liverpool and Hamburg

they could find a drummer. Pete Best was the son of Mona Best, who ran a youth club in the cellar of her house where the Beatles would occasionally play for fifteen shillings each a night. Pete had just left one group and was looking for another. Yes, he would come to Hamburg.

The visit to Hamburg was an eye-opening experience for a group of teenagers who had hardly ever left home before. They found they had to play for up to six hours a night in a cellar full of drunks and fights; they were paid so little that they could barely afford to eat; and their living quarters were a squalid little room behind a cinema screen, where the sound of the films hardly ever allowed them any sleep.

But they began to learn how to be a professional group, playing as loud as they could and singing at the tops of their voices to make themselves heard over the din of an audience which was more interested in drinking than listening to music. They put their heart and soul into their act, belting out their songs in a frenzy, for fear that if the audience did not like them they might invade the tiny stage and attack them.

While they were there they made their first record, of *Fever* and *Summertime*, in a little coin-in-the-slot recording booth on Hamburg railway station. It was just for fun, and no more was ever heard about it.

The Beatles had been in Hamburg for four months, when disaster struck. The German police found out that George Harrison was only seventeen, and therefore too young to work in a night club. He was put on the first plane back to England, and the others followed several days later. It looked like the end of their professional career.

Paul arrived home at Forthlin Road in Liverpool utterly exhausted, and as thin as a coathanger. And there was more bad news; his examination results arrived to tell him that although he had passed in art, he had failed in English. It was the end of Jim McCartney's hopes that his son would become a schoolteacher, and the start of Paul's wondering what on earth he would do next.

5 The Cavern

When he came home from Hamburg, Paul was not at all sure that he wanted to become a professional musician. He loved music above all else, but he knew that it was a very uncertain and sometimes rough life. Paul was a boy who wanted to succeed at something, so that his family and friends would look up and admire him.

He was still only eighteen years old. For a few months he took a succession of odd jobs, delivering parcels or working in a steel mill. But in the end the music won; he had it in his blood, and he was not truly happy unless he was performing in front of an audience. He and John Lennon decided to revive the Beatles, and to search Merseyside for work.

Dance hall owners in those days always had big bands which played 'proper' dance music for the waltz, foxtrot or quickstep. Occasionally they might play a rock tune as a novelty number. But the dance hall owners of Liverpool quickly realised that there was money to be made from the beat music craze. They began to hire beat groups to play at their dances, and the Beatles soon found themselves with regular bookings, not least because they were able to advertise themselves as 'direct from Hamburg', which made them sound much more famous than they really were. Everyone who knew them remarked how much better they were playing since their gruelling four-month stint in Germany.

The dance hall owners did not like the beat dances, and held them only because they brought in money.

The songs of Paul and John live on long after the break-up of the Beatles

Too often they attracted teddy boys and hooligans, and fights would break out. Even the bands were attacked if the audience did not like their music. On one occasion the Beatles were attacked while leaving a dance hall, and Stuart Sutcliffe was kicked to the ground with a heavy blow from a boot on his head.

Ray McFall was another man who did not care for beat music, but thought it might be good for business. He owned a jazz club called the Cavern, in a dank and musty cellar under a warehouse in Mathew Street, Liverpool. True jazz lovers would never listen to beat, but perhaps a beat session at lunchtimes would bring in the office workers for an hour.

In January 1961 McFall hired the Beatles, and in just over a year they played 292 times at his club, for twenty-five shillings each (£1.25) a day. Because they had become well known at dances all over Merseyside, their fans followed them to the Cavern and filled the tiny cellar so full that it was almost impossible to breathe. There was one simple reason why, of all the groups in Liverpool, they already had the biggest following: the Beatles were different.

Liverpool groups were different from London groups. Liverpool was a big seaport, full of seamen from the great liners who travelled regularly to America, and were known as the 'Cunard Yanks', after the famous shipping line. When in America, the seamen would hear the raw, original rhythm and blues music on which rock and roll was based, and they would bring back records of singers like Chuck Berry.

Elsewhere in the country, young people were listening to British beat music, which was sweeter and more tuneful than the original hard rock. In fact, even parents and grandparents could sometimes be heard to say that really, Cliff Richard was not *too* bad at all. But Paul and John, and their Liverpool fans, preferred the rough, loud, exciting rhythm and blues, arranging the songs in their own way and even writing their own in the same style. Then they belted them out with all that energy and drive they had learned in Hamburg.

The Beatles' appearance was different, too. Other beat groups liked to wear neat suits and ties and some, like the Shadows, even performed dance steps as they played. The Beatles dressed in black leather and scruffy tennis shoes, and leapt all over the stage while they delivered their songs at the tops of their voices.

In the summer of 1961, while at the Cavern, they were invited back to Hamburg to play in a club for £40

Cliff Richard, here with two fan club members, was one of Britain's early 'home-grown' rock singers

a week each, more than double what they had ever earned before.

When they came back they had money in their pockets, and Paul was able to buy his first car, a second-hand Ford Classic. But while they were in Hamburg, something much more significant happened. They were asked to perform as the backing group on a record by another British singer, Tony Sheridan, who sang a rock version of *My Bonnie Lies Over the Ocean*. The record sold very badly, but somehow a few copies found their way back to Liverpool, and word of it flew around the Beatles' fans.

One day a customer walked into North End Music Stores, the largest record shop in Liverpool, and asked for *My Bonnie* by the Beatles. The manager, Brian Epstein, had never heard of it; he had never even heard of the Beatles. But when a second customer the same day asked for the same record, he thought he had better find out who this strange unknown group were.

6 Sorry, no Guitars

On the tiny stage of the Cavern Club, Brian Epstein saw four young men in scruffy black leather who jumped about in all directions and argued with the audience. But even Brian, who came from a respectable Jewish home and always wore smart suits, could see that their music was powerful, exciting, and like nothing else he had ever heard.

There was Paul, with his round young face and his voice so high that he sounded almost like a girl. There was John, mean and angry looking; George, who now as a permanent member of the group was struggling hard to improve his guitar playing; and Pete Best on drums, whom all the girls thought was the most handsome of the four.

There was no Stuart Sutcliffe. He had decided to stay behind in Hamburg and return to being an art student. Paul was glad; he regarded Stuart as a poor player, and anyway he wanted the position of bass guitar for himself. Now he had it. Not long afterwards Stuart died in Hamburg from a brain haemorrhage, probably a result of that kick in the head at the dance hall fight.

Brian could see immediately that John and Paul were the real leaders of the group, John the rebel and Paul the musician. He could see too that Paul was a singer with a wide range, from rhythm and blues 'screamers' like *Long Tall Sally* to gentle love ballads like *Till There Was You*. Would they, Brian asked them, allow him to be their manager, to look after them and find them dates, in return for a quarter of everything they earned? He went to see Jim McCartney, a good Roman Catholic, who was not sure about his son, still only twenty, being looked after by a Jewish manager. He assured Jim that his son would be properly taken care of. Very well, said Jim. Very well, said the Beatles.

The first thing Brian insisted upon was that they smarten themselves up, and he bought them matching suits from Burtons the tailors to wear on stage. He let them keep their funny mop-head haircuts which they had had done on their last visit to Hamburg.

Paul was the only one to agree readily to the band's new image; he was in favour of anything that would make them more popular. John would have been quite happy to remain in his old black leather jacket.

But what their new manager really wanted was for them to make a record. The Beatles were a popular and well known group in Liverpool, but no one had ever

Brian Epstein managed the Beatles during their first years of world-wide success

Being turned down after their first recording test was a big disappointment for the Beatles

heard of them anywhere else in the country. A hit record, Brian decided, was the only way that they would become *really* famous.

Being a record shop manager, Brian knew all the right people to approach, and he went to London with a tape of the Beatles playing at the Cavern under his arm. But he met with no success at all. 'Sorry', all the record companies told him, 'Beat music is finished. We don't want groups with guitars any more. We want solo singers with big orchestras now.' Later, he went back to London and tried again. This time Decca, one of the biggest record companies, agreed to give the group an audition.

On New Year's Day 1962 the group crammed themselves and their instruments into a tiny van and drove through the snow to London for their audition. The men at Decca thought they were *quite* good, but no better than dozens of other hopeful groups. 'Sorry', said the men at Decca, and signed up Brian Poole and the Tremeloes from Dagenham instead.

The dejected Beatles left England for another stint in the night clubs of Hamburg. But Brian did not give up. Armed with a copy of *Mersey Beat*, the Liverpool music newspaper which had published a poll showing the Beatles were the most popular group in the city, he went to London yet again, and this time he struck gold. He met a record producer called George Martin, who worked for EMI, the biggest record company of all, and played him the Beatles tape. 'Hmmm', said Martin, 'there *might* just be something there.'

Once again the group set off for London, to display their talents to Martin in the Abbey Road recording studios in north London. They performed *Love Me Do*, a song which John and Paul had written, and a few old standards, like *Red Sails In The Sunset*, given the full Beatles treatment. Martin liked what he heard, with one exception: he did not think Pete Best's drumming was up to the standard of the rest of the group. Could they find another drummer?

On 11 September 1962 the group returned to Abbey Road to make the final version of *Love Me Do* with, on the other side, *P.S. I Love You*, specially chosen to show off Paul's voice. With them they brought Richard Starkey, a drummer they had first met in Hamburg when he played for another Liverpool group, Rory Storm and the Hurricanes. Starkey had changed his

Ringo Starr was brought in as drummer for the Beatles' first record, and stayed

name to Starr, and because he wore so many rings on his fingers his friends called him Ringo.

Love Me Do was released on 4 October, and for every copy sold at six shillings and eightpence (33p) the Beatles were to receive one old penny (less than ½p) — not one penny each; one penny divided among the four.

7   Beatlemania

When *Love Me Do* was issued, Brian Epstein bought 10,000 copies for his own Liverpool shop. Of course the record sold well in the Beatles' home town, but elsewhere it was only a modest success, creeping briefly into the Top Thirty.

It was their second record, another song by John and Paul called *Please Please Me*, which was to make them famous. They were in Hamburg when it was issued in January 1963, but they returned home quickly when they were offered an appearance on the most important pop music television show of the time, *Thank Your Lucky Stars.*

People suddenly began to take notice. Newspapers wrote about them because they were different. They did not dress like other groups, they did not dance in step while they played, they had funny mop-head haircuts, and they were cheeky and cheerful, full of the sharp jokes that Liverpudlians are famous for. By March the record had reached number one, and for the next four years every record they made did exactly the same.

The Liverpool Sound had arrived, and record buyers could not get enough of it. Brian Epstein signed up other local groups, like Gerry and the Pacemakers and Billy J. Kramer and the Dakotas, and if John and Paul could be persuaded to write songs for them, they too went straight to the top of the charts.

The Beatles went on a tour of Britain, and everywhere they stopped to give a concert, they heard the

Gerry and the Pacemakers were another Brian Epstein group who found success with the 'Liverpool Sound'

same deafening sound. It was the sound of girls screaming with excitement, and the newspapers invented a word for it — Beatlemania. When they appeared in the Royal Variety Performance at the London Palladium in November 1963, fifteen million television viewers heard John tell the rich and important audience: 'You in the cheap seats can clap; the rest of you just rattle your jewelry.'

Now that they were nationally famous, Brian decided that they should all move to London. Paul finally left his childhood home at Forthlin Road. His father was sad to see him go, but relieved too: the fans had found out where Paul lived, and they had been camping on Jim McCartney's doorstep day and night. Paul could not even have his twenty-first birthday party at home because of the fans in the street outside: he had to sneak over to his aunt's house in Birkenhead.

The Beatles achieved national fame at the Royal Variety Performance

In London, Paul lived at first at the home of Sir Richard Asher, a famous doctor, whose daughter Jane had become his girl friend. Later he bought himself a large house at St John's Wood in north London, with security locks on the garden gates. But the fans learned how to open them, and sometimes they would even manage to get inside the house to steal souvenirs.

It was annoying for Paul, but it showed how remarkably popular the Beatles were. Their music was just right for the times. These were the Swinging Sixties, the period when the people of Britain enjoyed a short spell of real peace and prosperity, when jobs were plenty and people had money to spend. Scandals in the newspapers about politicians convinced young people that their leaders were just a lot of feeble old men. Bright, catchy, not too serious music sung by a group full of jokes and wit, was just what young people wanted.

It was the same in America, where people needed cheering up after their young and popular president, John Kennedy, had been murdered as he drove through Dallas, Texas. When the Beatles first arrived in America in 1964, thousands of people mobbed them at the airport, and at one time Beatles records occupied all five top places in the American Top Hundred chart.

For nearly four years the life of Paul and the other Beatles was an endless and exhausting round of concerts, British and world tours, films, personal appearances and recording sessions. They saw almost nothing except the insides of countless heavily-guarded hotel rooms, backstage dressing-rooms, and audiences numbered in thousands. They could have no life of their own. To walk alone in the street would have meant being mobbed by the fans, and quite possibly being crushed to death.

In his few spare moments when he was not writing songs, Paul did manage one thing he had been meaning to do for years; he went back to learning the piano.

But the strain was beginning to tell on them. They became terrified of the huge crowds which surrounded them, and of having to be snatched from theatres by cordons of armed police. Riots and fights would

Paul's long-standing girlfriend, Jane Asher, became a successful actress

sometimes break out at their concerts, and Paul was often physically sick with fear before going on stage.

Worst of all, the audiences no longer listened to their music; they just screamed, and they screamed so loudly that the four Beatles could not hear themselves play. They had just finished a concert in San Francisco on 29 August 1966, when they made a decision; they would never appear in public again.

8   Singing for Pennies

The first thing that Paul did when the touring stopped was to take a long holiday, driving across Africa with his friend and road manager, Mal Evans. Nearly four years of being one of the four best known faces in the world had exhausted him, and he needed time to rest, recover and reflect.

So much had happened in those four years: twelve hit singles from *Please Please Me* to *Eleanor Rigby*, all of them written by himself and John; seven albums, all of them huge hits, from *Please Please Me* to *Revolver*; medals from the new Labour Prime Minister, Harold Wilson, who thought it would be a clever way to attract young voters.

And for Paul himself, who four years before had lived in the modest family home at Forthlin Road and driven an old Ford, there was now a big house in St John's Wood, a large sheep farm he had bought on the Mull of Kintyre on the west coast of Scotland, and two brand new cars, a white Aston Martin and a special extra-fast Mini.

Yet for all their success, Paul and the other Beatles were not nearly as rich as people imagined. They were still getting only a penny for every record they sold, and although they had sold millions, millions of pennies divided among four is not *that* much money. Their concert tours were enormously expensive to organize, what with hiring aircraft, the best hotels, and squads of security guards, and often the money they made only just covered their cost.

Former Prime Minister, Harold Wilson, tried to win young people's votes by having MBEs awarded to the Beatles

But a lot of other people made a great deal of money out of the Beatles. The record company made huge profits, the concert promoters greedily counted their takings, and the businessmen who gave companies permission to make Beatle souvenirs made fortunes for doing next to nothing, while the Beatles got only ten pence (4p) for every pound's worth sold. Paul and John did not even own the songs they wrote, and if another singer wanted to record one of them, once again it was a businessman who collected most of the money.

There was worse to come. One day in the summer of 1967 the Beatles were attending a course in meditation in North Wales when Paul happened to walk by a ringing telephone. He picked it up to hear the news that their manager, Brian Epstein, had been found dead in his flat. His five-year contract to manage the group was coming to an end, and in his private life he was a very lonely man. It was as though he felt there was nothing left for him to do.

The Beatles entered the hippie era by forming their own Company, Apple

Although the Beatles had stopped performing in public, they could not stop making music. That same summer they made what their fans thought was their best album of all, *Sergeant Pepper's Lonely Hearts Club Band*, which sold four million copies. And Paul was still writing marvellous songs like *Penny Lane*, about places he remembered from his Liverpool childhood, and *Hey Jude*, written for John Lennon's son Julian.

With Brian gone the Beatles decided to set up their own company, Apple, to run their affairs and keep their money out of the hands of what John Lennon angrily called 'the men in suits'. But Apple was a disaster. It was badly run, and huge sums of money were spent on expensive lunches, or even given away to people who came to the door with a hard-luck story. The Beatles themselves no longer seemed to know which way they were going. In 1968 they spent nine weeks in India meditating with the Maharishi Mahesh Yogi, who claimed to be a kind of holy man and who

43

was delighted to have such famous people in his movement.

They made two more albums, *White Album* and *Yellow Submarine*, but the fans thought they were very poor compared with the records they used to make. And there were new heroes for young people to listen to, performers like Bob Dylan who sang angry songs of protest against war, and the Rolling Stones, who unlike the Beatles were definitely *not* approved of by parents and grandparents.

They were struggling to make a combined film and album to be called *Let It Be*, but it was taking a very long time. Nothing would work properly, and the four argued constantly. Paul was not popular with the others, as he was always ordering them about, trying to get the film made. Their enthusiasm had gone; they were no longer interested. It was only Paul who wanted to keep the Beatles together.

Eventually Paul suggested that they should make one last album, the way they used to make them, in their old style. He really wanted them all to go on tour again, as he was beginning to miss the excitement of live concerts, but the others would have nothing to do with it. They did, however, agree to return to Abbey Road studios, and their old record producer George Martin, for one final recording session. It was the last time the Beatles ever performed together, and the record was called simply *Abbey Road*. It sold five million copies, more than any other Beatles record.

Soon after it was issued in October 1969, Paul surprised his fans by marrying, not Jane Asher, his girl

The Beatles travelled to India to meditate at the school of the
Maharishi Mahesh Yogi

friend from the early days in London, but Linda
Eastman, an American photographer. Linda, as it
turned out, was to prove very useful to Paul — her
father and her brother John were clever and experienced
lawyers.

Paul wanted John Eastman to come to London and
sort out the dreadful mess that the Apple company had
got itself into, but the other three wanted Allen Klein,
another American who looked after the Rolling Stones.
The others won, and Klein arrived. Although he was
eventually sacked by the Beatles he did manage to
recover for them more than one million pounds they
had been owed in fees.

Paul finally married Linda Eastman, the daughter of an American lawyer

There was one last Beatles album to be released, the hours of rambling and disjointed tapes that had finally been edited and issued as *Let It Be*. The film was shown in London, but on the opening night the Beatles were nowhere to be seen. They had finally parted, and months before Paul had disappeared to the privacy of his Scottish farm. He kept so quiet that some people began to say he was dead.

9 Flying Solo

At High Park Farm, near Campbeltown on the west coast of Scotland, Paul was very far from dead. In fact, after the last unhappy years of the Beatles, he was beginning to live again. He was glad to be alone with his wife Linda and new baby daughter Mary, driving his tractor, planting vegetables, shearing sheep, and practising his talent for drawing and painting.

Most important of all, he was hard at work on a new record album all by himself. Paul was anxious to prove to himself and to everyone else that he did not need the Beatles, that he could be a performer in his own right. He asked the Apple company to issue the album, called simply *McCartney*, in April 1970, but they refused, saying it would clash with the Beatles' final record, *Let It Be*. It was the last straw. Paul, who had tried so hard to keep the Beatles together, now determined to break them up, finally and forever.

With the help of his brother-in-law, John Eastman, Paul started proceedings in the High Court to have the Apple company shut down. He had never liked the new boss, Allen Klein, even although Klein had managed to get the Beatles much, much more money for every one of their records sold than they had done in the bad old penny-a-time days. Now they got a quarter of what you paid in the shop for each of their singles and albums. And their records were to go on selling in millions for years to come.

Paul's solo album was eventually issued, but it was a tremendous flop. 'Paul is nothing without the Beatles', the critics jeered. 'Very well', thought Paul, 'I'll form a band of my own.'

He began with Linda, who had not played music since she had been at school. Paul was keen to involve her in his work, and he patiently taught her simple piano chords. He hired an experienced drummer, and the three tried again, with an album called *Ram*. Again it was a disaster. 'Very well', thought Paul, 'I'll have a bigger band.' And he hired two more experienced guitarists. 'What shall we call it?' he asked Linda while she was in hospital having their next daughter, Stella. 'I think Wings of Angels would be a good name.' 'Why not just Wings?' suggested Linda. So it was Wings who made an album called *Wildlife*, and once again the critics and the record buyers said enormously rude things about it.

Paul has always been very determined that everything he does should be a success, and he was not going to give up that easily. He realised that Wings needed experience, which meant playing in front of live audiences again. But he was afraid that they were not really good enough, and he was also afraid that people might come to see them just because their lead singer was a former Beatle. What they really wanted was to play some concerts in secret, which is not easy when the whole idea of a concert is to attract an audience.

Early in 1972 Paul and Linda, their children and dogs, the band and their instruments, squeezed into a caravan and set off from Campbeltown without telling anyone where they were going. They drove to Nottingham University and sent their road manager

After their trial run at British universities, Paul and Linda took the Wings band
on a tour of Europe

into the students' union to ask if they could play. The students were astonished when they saw who walked out on to the stage.

Paul was very nervous, for he had not played to a live audience for six years. Linda was equally nervous, for she had never played to a live audience in her life, and she was not even a professional musician, which made the professional musicians in the band very angry indeed. Paul would not tolerate any criticism of her.

For two weeks they toured the universities of Britain, arriving unannounced and asking if they could perform on the spot. The adventure was a modest success, and they were encouraged to make a tour of Europe. Paul decided that the band's playing had greatly improved; even Linda was now hitting the right notes. 'We're ready', said Paul, 'to make a successful record.' Once again, he wrote a whole collection of new songs for it, as he had done for all the previous albums. He was determined not to rely on singing old Beatles hits, and he turned out fresh songs by the dozen. But *Red Rose Speedway* was just as big a flop as all the previous albums.

Things were going very badly for Paul: two members of the band told him they were leaving because they could not work with him any more. He was too bossy, they said. That, Paul vowed, was not going to prevent him having one last try at making a hit album. To capture a new and more exciting atmosphere the three remaining members of Wings — Paul, Linda and Denny Laine — flew to Africa to make the record.

While they were in Lagos in Nigeria they were

The final line-up of Wings was just three — Paul, Linda and
guitarist Denny Laine

attacked and robbed, and Paul fell ill with fever, but
out of the seeming chaos and disaster emerged the
album *Band On The Run*. 'Brilliant!' chorused the critics
at last. It sold six million copies, more than any Beatles
record had ever done, and three of the tracks became
hit singles on their own. Paul McCartney had finally
made it without the Beatles.

Wings continued to have its ups and downs. It was
not a band like the Beatles, who in their heyday seemed
to turn everything they touched to gold. Musicians
came and went; occasionally their records flopped; and
a planned tour of Japan had to be cancelled when the
Japanese refused to let Paul into their country because
they knew he smoked drugs.

But on the whole, Wings became a huge commercial
success after *Band On The Run*. Their tours were packed

out, and most of their records sold in millions. Yet they did not attract the hysterical screaming that the Beatles had done. People actually listened to the music.

In May, 1976, at a concert in Seattle in the United States, a total of 67,100 people bought tickets for the huge hall to hear Paul and the Wings band play. It was the largest audience there had ever been for an indoor concert by a single band, anywhere in the world.

10 Silly Love Songs

In the spring of 1977 Paul cancelled his tours and concerts to be at home on his farm for the birth of his third child, James. He loved his Scottish home so much that he decided to write a song about it. Wanting it to be a Scottish-sounding song, he recorded it with the help of the local pipe band at Campbeltown, and he named it after the tip of the long, narrow neck of the Scottish coast that lies just to the south of High Park Farm. *Mull of Kintyre* shot straight to the top of the charts and stayed there for four months, to become the biggest selling single record in British history, at well over two million copies.

From the sale of that record, and from the sale of no fewer than 100 million Wings albums around the world, Paul could easily have afforded to retire; he had already earned more money than he could ever possibly need. But he was a born musician, who needed to perform, and there were still some things he badly wanted to do. For example, he wanted to take Wings to Japan, because they had never been allowed to go there, even though the Japanese bought more pop records than anyone except the Americans. So in 1980 he, Linda and Denny Laine arrived at Tokyo airport to begin a major tour of that country.

But as they entered the terminal, their luck ran out. The customs officers opened their luggage to find large quantities of drugs. Paul was immediately arrested and put in jail, where he remained for ten of the most frightening days of his life. As soon as he was released the band had to leave the country and come home. The tour of Japan had collapsed, and it was their own fault.

That year was to bring one more appalling shock to Paul, and to millions of pop music lovers all over the world. On 8 December, outside an apartment block in New York, John Lennon was shot dead. It was the sad, bitter and final end of a partnership which had begun twenty-three years before at a church fete in Liverpool and had blossomed into one of the greatest partnerships popular music had ever seen.

Paul was shattered by the loss of his friend, although in recent years they had not spoken much, and when they did they often quarrelled. He was also very frightened and wondered if such a dreadful thing could happen to John, could it also happen to Paul? He hired burly security guards to protect him day and night, and finally decided that the Wings band must be broken up because he felt too afraid to go on tour again. Another remarkable chapter in Paul's life had closed.

But nothing can stop Paul writing and performing, and he continues to make albums on his own, although the songs he writes now are nothing like those he wrote when John Lennon was there to spark him off. They are not angry songs, or songs of protest, or deep, heart-touching songs of unhappiness. They are romantic, pretty songs, and one of them is even about the kind of music he writes, called *Silly Love Songs*. Paul has never lost his genius for writing catchy and appealing melodies, and he can still create the kind of music that the public will buy by the million.

After seeing how much of the Beatles' earnings

Paul is a devoted father and family man

slipped through their fingers, Paul has learned to be very canny with his own fortune. He has become a very rich man indeed, not only through the sale of Wings records, and Beatles records which still sell twelve years after the group was broken up. Every time anyone, anywhere, plays a Beatles record or a Wings record on radio or juke box, or any McCartney song is recorded by any singer, Paul receives a payment.

Soon after he was married, his father-in-law advised him to invest his money wisely, and if music was what he liked and knew about, then that was where he should invest it. Paul has become the owner of the songs of some other very famous composers, now dead, like Hoagy Carmichael and Buddy Holly, and every time one of *their* songs is sung or played, he receives a payment. He has also bought the rights to several hit musical shows, including *Hello Dolly, Chorus Line, Annie* and *Grease*, and every time one of *those* is performed Paul receives a payment.

There is one thing which he would very much like to own, and has spent years trying to buy. In the bad old days of the Beatles, most of the money Paul and John should have earned as the composers of all those hit songs went to 'the men in suits' whom John so hated. Paul was never able to buy them back, but he has always felt they properly belong to him.

As a performer travelling the world, Paul has had all the excitement he could ever wish, and he is now devoted to his family life with Linda, their three children, and Linda's daughter Heather by her previous marriage. Paul almost spends more time as a farmer nowadays than as a musician; as well as his Scottish farm he has another near Rye in Sussex, where the family spend most of the year.

He owns two other houses, his mansion in St John's Wood which he bought when the Beatles first became successful, and another in his home city of Liverpool. Paul is still very close to his family and he has never forgotten the roots from which he came and which provided him with so much inspiration for his music.

Above all else, he is still a musician, an accomplished player of guitar, keyboards and drums, who cannot stop performing or writing his songs. Even after the disbanding of Wings he has continued to make number one hits like *Ebony and Ivory* with Stevie Wonder, and his albums like *Tug Of War* still sail effortlessly up the charts.

Unlike many pop stars who live ridiculously rich lives on tropical islands with solid gold bath taps and swimming pools big enough to tire a whale, Paul has

Paul the bandleader has also had great success as a solo performer

Paul is never short of work to do on his two farms in Sussex and Scotland

tried hard to remain ordinary. He is a vegetarian; he will not allow animals, even the rabbits which nibble his crops, to be killed on his farms. He sends his children to the local school, while Linda spends much of her time, like any other mother, in the kitchen, although she also works as a professional photographer.

Like any other businessman, Paul travels to London most days to be at the office of his music publishing company in Soho Square, or at a recording studio.

But Paul McCartney is not ordinary. No ordinary man would have the talent, the determination, the capacity for sheer hard work, and the luck, to become one of the most successful songwriters and performers there has ever been. And knowing Paul, he will probably go on making music until the day he dies.